The Unseen

Paul Melniczek

The Unseen

Paul Melniczek

King's Way Press
Atlanta 2018

King's Way Press

4215 Jimmy Lee Smith Pkwy.
Suite 19-210
Hiram GA 30141
http://www.kwp-books.com

978-0-9988367-3-7

The Unseen

Paul Melniczek

Paul Melniczek

The Unseen

Prologue

THE BOY STEPPED CAUTIOUSLY ACROSS THE SMALL stream, *careful not to slip on the wet rocks. Halfway over, he paused, his dreamy blue eyes gazing into a pool which nestled against gnarled oak roots. Something dark stirred within the shallow depths, and he watched as a flash of silver darted between the protective arms of its haven, a fish of some unknown species, larger than any he'd ever seen in the creek before.*

Mesmerized, he lowered himself, trying not to scare the fish away. He searched for movement, hoping to catch another glimpse, fascinated that something of this size could live in such a small stream. The air around him was filled with an earthy aroma of damp soil and decaying leaves. The forest had a unique smell of its own, of the growing things that lived there, and also died there as well. He caught fragrances of decay and mold, and despite his young years, he already understood that everything had its proper place in the world, and there could be no summer without winter, no light without dark, no life without death. There existed a balance both wonderful and terrible.

While his youthful mind harbored these adult thoughts, he noticed another smell now, something out of place beneath the gentle eaves of the forest. It was a strong odor, one that spoke of crackling wood and licking flames.

It smelled like a fire.

But where was it coming from, he wondered? There were no houses or cabins nearby, and he had never seen hikers or other people in this part of the mountain. This property belonged to his family.

Ignoring his hidden quarry altogether, he straightened, craning his neck about, attempting to locate the source of the fire. A breeze stirred the leaves and twigs surrounding him, and the smell of smoke was powerful. He turned his head across the stream and toward the trees which blanketed his scope of vision, and a chill of fear traveled along his spine when he realized where the source of fire came from...

His home.

Eyes opening in fright, he bounded over the remaining rocks, not caring anymore if his shoes became wet. He crashed ahead, running along the narrow deer path which he used, passing by bushes and clumps of trees, all the time the smell growing stronger and stronger, until minutes later the forest gave way and opened wide before him, revealing an open hilltop carpeted by green, the grass rolling towards a cyclonic inferno of orange and yellow, an angry and malicious bonfire which fed hungrily on the timbers of his house.

Horrified, he was frozen where he stood. Never

had he seen such a nightmarish image in all his waking (and sleeping) years. His eyes watered from the acrid smoke, combining with the terror which held him fast, and he searched desperately for any sign that his parents were somewhere outside -- anywhere -- and not still trapped within the deadly flames.

His entire body was numb, and he fought wildly to bring himself into action. The restraining bonds of his immobility snapped and he plunged ahead, running heedlessly towards his home. He screamed at the top of his lungs, all the while choking on the oppressive smoke which threatened to smother the life from his chest. The heat was intense, and grew with every step closer. The backdoor was closed, and the front porch was engulfed in a storm of gray fog, sparks showering the afternoon sunlight like miniature enraged comets.

There could be no escape from the entrance, so he ran to the back, reaching the steps within seconds, screaming for his parents. What had happened? Where were they?

There were no answers to his questions, and no time to think, only time to act. He grabbed the doorknob, wincing from the heat as it burned his hand. But he never even had a chance to go inside as the support beams heaved and shifted, the very foundations of the house succumbing to the fire and violence. He looked up as the roof of the porch collapsed, one beam coming down hard and pinning him to the floorboards. He felt a vise of pain grip his chest and all the air left him in one terrible rush. Still conscious, he struggled to free himself, but the weight of the beam was too much for his young muscles, and he knew instantly that it would be impossible for him to escape. He gasped, trying to breathe, scream words of warning and help, but no sound left his lips. He was too young to die. It wasn't fair...He saw the sun shining through the smog and he pleaded with it to save him, teased by the mirage of something gentle and normal, a paradoxical vision of hope far removed from the chaos which claimed him as victim.

How could this all have happened? And why? Where were his parents?

But he knew the answer, and felt the appalling irony of the truth -- that they had been inside, taken by surprise, and were still there. And here he was, also trapped, but on the outside of the home, unable to escape their fate. They'd always been close as a family, spending precious time together, sharing their hopes, dreams, and joys. He pictured his mother's tender and loving face, his father's kind eyes and sturdy brow.

Close in life. Now they would continue that connection, but this time locked in death. Fate was a cruel and terrible thing, the ultimate enactor of cause and consequence -- unforgiving, unfeeling, and uncaring.

The end was near and the flames danced closer, their silhouettes taking on dreadful forms. He knew it was his time, but he wept inside, angry that things had happened so swiftly and violently, rearing up to snuff out the lives of his parents and himself in one freak accident. It wasn't fair. Nothing could be so unfair...

Pushing with the last of his strength, he knew his situation was hopeless. They lived too far from town, and by the time a rescue group would arrive, they would only find the charred remains of the family who had lived there so peacefully, so happily...

His skin seared from the heat, he prepared for the end, as the fire reached an incredible level of intensity. Too much for anyone to overcome.

Eyes facing skywards, his face contorted into a look of sheer horror as he saw a huge form tower over him, something monstrous, born of nightmares. In shock,

The Unseen

his mouth opened wide as it came closer, and he wished himself dead, fearing that he already was...

And then a great weight eased off his chest, the fire fell away, and he lost consciousness.

Paul Melniczek

The Unseen

Chapter One

Late spring had arrived in full bloom in the town of Trackville. Honeysuckle and lilac scents trailed across the air, sweet and relaxing. Dandelions dotted the grassy banks like tiny splashes of golden sun stolen from the heavens. Lewis sat against an ancient oak tree, the great trunk lunging forward hungrily as it leaned precariously over Sparse River, the roots protruding from the ground like the tentacles of an enraged octopus. He pushed his hat back an inch and rubbed his cheek, feeling the three day's growth of beard. He didn't like to shave, and wasn't one for routines of any kind regardless. It was a nuisance, and one that had little bearing on his life, whether he was shaven or overgrown.

The water was wide but flowed lazily at this point, directly below the bridge which spanned its course, serving as the main roadway into the quiet town. Iron trestling over concrete foundations, it was a postcard vision of tranquility. Built to last, it had seasoned many years. The road plunged between jagged peaks and forested valleys, veining off several miles away from the nearby interstate, as it encroached on a region thrown back from the beaten path. There were few visitors from out of town to speak of. A handful of hikers during the fall, distant relatives of the native inhabitants, and occasional drifters coming from nowhere, heading to nowhere. Time had forgotten this area, and for good reason. The place suffered little intrusion from the outside world, and nearly everyone in the sleepy little city preferred it that way. On appearance, Trackville was a typical Pennsylvanian town south of the Pocono Mountains, nothing special, its claim to fame evident from the residue of the gutted coal mines, the sizable mounds of excavated rock encircling the area like giant, watchful, shapeless guardians awakened from the deep caverns of the earth far below. Coal had once been king, but had relinquished its crown a long while ago, and wasn't coming back for its throne any time soon.

Lewis had little interest in the history of his hometown, or its future, for that matter. Right now, his mind was entirely focused on his current undertaking. He stared intently at his solitary fishing rod, eyes alert for any telltale tapping of the line, signaling an excited and hungry fish somewhere in the depths below. When he was younger, he used to wonder what lurked in the hidden waters deep at the bottom. But things had happened that changed his curiosity over time.

Now he *knew* what was down there…and anywhere else which harbored dark secrets, whether it be deep water, the depths of abandoned coal mines, or the nightmares of men.

The Unseen

He was content to just sit there and let the day roll along, not bothering anyone, and not to be bothered himself. Then again, it was pretty much the norm for him. He looked upwards, closing his eyes. His black hair was cut short, if a bit crooked, as he did the honors himself. Almost entirely independent, Lewis made trips into town on an 'as needed' basis, but had ended most of his social interaction with the townsfolk some time back. Circumstances had forced it to be this way. Often he regretted it, and he couldn't help but to wonder one single, powerful thought.

Why him?

He exhaled, squirming to the left as a tree knot chiseled a tiny hole into his back. Shifting into a more comfortable posture, he sighed, breathing deeply, rearranging his dismal thoughts. He was simply enjoying the warm day, and nothing was going to change that. Not the past, not the present, and certainly not the future. A pair of geese glided ambiguously over the water, and he spotted a large bullfrog near the edge where the river pooled up, the current swirling idly back on itself beneath the looming framework of the pillars supporting the bridge. The central arch stood like a testament to time, just another structure on the long list for state inspection. One more thing for the townspeople to grumble about, although there was hardly any rush hour, and the temporary lane closures would inconvenience few. Lewis understood all this, of course, but he also understood the mentality of the small town. As a whole, it was charming in its own way and pleasant enough, as long as one fit in…

Acceptance. Something which he would never need to worry about, both the good and the bad that went along with it.

Lewis lifted his head as he heard voices coming from the other side of the river.

Paul Melniczek

Several figures approached, and he recognized one or two faces. They were men from the hat factory upstream, usual suspects to hit the waters after their shift was done, ready for some R&R, with a fishing rod in one hand, a cold beer in the other...They pretty much ignored Lewis, although one of them waved a hand and yelled something, sounding friendly enough. Lewis raised a hand in return, completing the formality and leaving it at that. They always fished on that side of the river, and he always stuck to his spot on this one. If they ever had a mind to come over, well, then he would move elsewhere. Simple solution, and no big deal in itself.

The men laughed and joked, passing around a large cooler and pulling out several bottles, cracking them open and handing them out. Lewis felt a bit uncomfortable and envied them, longing for the companionship that was denied to him. As always, the feeling quickly melted away, and he glanced around, his eyes looking for something nearby.

A rumbling came from across the stream, and the familiar roar of the school bus interrupted his thinking for a moment. The time had to be around 3:30, the bus returning into town to unload its young occupants. Lewis fondly recalled his own childhood, the early days. The ones filled with games and pranks, the close comradeship of his fellow classmates, the majority who viewed their schooling as an unwelcome incarceration. Things hadn't been *quite* that bad, true, but still, they'd viewed themselves as victims of an unfair judgment, forced to attend and do their part. Lewis figured most kids still felt the same way these days. He was in his mid-twenties; had things changed that much since then? Well, some things *definitely*. But the mindset of an overactive teenager? Probably not...Why learn when there was plenty of loafing to do? And these days, the toys were a lot better and cooler. Playstations and DVD

16

burners, cellphones and all those other trendy gadgets. Lewis didn't need any of it, but that didn't mean everyone else was like him. That much he knew for fact.

He lost himself in memory fragments for a moment, recalling the old school day songs.

The driver blows the school bus horn, with a honk and a...

Hmm, Lewis couldn't remember the rest of the words, only the melody of the plainsong, lapping around in his head like a warped 45 record. He still had some of those at home. *No 8-tracks though...*

Deep, blue sea, baby, deep blue sea.

Deep, blue sea, baby, sing to me...

Deep, blue sea, baby, deep blue sea.

It was Willy, what got drown-dead, in the deep, blue sea...

As if on cue with the tune playing in his mind, a tremendous cracking sound echoed across the valley, and Lewis snapped his head up, startled. His mouth dropped open as he heard the screech of tires skidding, protesting the unexpected pounding of brakes, and he watched in shock as the school bus fishtailed, a huge part of the bridge caving in, great chunks dropping into the river like discards from a concrete glacier.

The bridge was collapsing...

The men across from him yelled out in helpless warning, but it was apparent to all the witnesses that fate held the reins in its cruel hands. It seemed impossible to Lewis that the peaceful warmth of the day could be shattered by such a terrible vision.

He gasped, horrified at the scene taking place before his eyes. And then the first of the screams started...

High-pitched, piercing his heart like a shaft of steel. Child voices, wailing in terror as they realized what was happening to them, and what must surely follow.

Lewis felt the skin freeze across his arms and back. Horror blanketed him, terrible and absolute. His throat constricted, and he found himself holding his breath. The bus was loaded with children returning to their homes in town. They didn't have a chance to escape. Everything was happening so fast, and the scene would reach its terrible conclusion in mere seconds.

The vehicle came to a complete stop, but the bridge was near total collapse. Huge splashes erupted from the river as debris continued to rain down from the crumbling structure like rocks thrown from great mountain giants. The men across from him waded into the water, some up to their chest, fighting the current, ready for whatever aid they could offer. But what could they possibly do? Lewis moved also, breaching the shallow water himself now, and he felt the terrible power of the moment like a physical vise, squeezing, suffocating him, until he was ready to burst. Death lurked quietly nearby, ready to claim victims.

He watched, feeling like he was an actor in a movie, unable to change the script, the action unfolding before his eyes. The bus perched there, teetering above the flowing water, an unfortunate part of uncontrollable events. One of the men stumbled onto the road looking for help, waving his arms frantically, the gesture making him appear like a scarecrow flapping in the breeze, as his flannel shirt whipped recklessly about. Long, precious seconds passed, and the structure imploded, the foundation severely undermined. The screams from the children grew to an earsplitting crescendo, and oddly, Lewis was reminded of a discordant opera he remembered listening to years ago, the harmonies eerie, the minor tones unsettling.

There was nowhere for the bus to go.

But down...

The Unseen

Before and behind, the road was devastated. Craters opened up everywhere, and the overhead support arch buckled uncertainly. It was only a matter of moments before everything collapsed, sending the remaining parts of the bridge into the river, along with its hapless victims.

Lewis was crushed. He held no animosity toward anyone in town, despite his self-appointed seclusion. The decision to remain aloof had always been his own, for reasons of his own. A social exile of sorts, although there were no clearly defined boundaries. He interacted in small ways, as needed. But this had nothing to do with how he now felt. These children were about to have their fragile lives snuffed out, and there was nothing that could save them in such a short time. He remembered a similar time as the shadow of his own past now reared up in his mind, as he had been helpless to save himself from a freak accident.

"Not again," he whispered.

The bus inched closer to the edge. The men shouted in alarm, their voices as shrill as the children's now.

Downstream, a bullfrog grunted.

Overhead, high clouds just missed the sun, the brightness of the day mocking the tragic events playing out below. Cool water lapped around his jeans, and Lewis felt the knot in his stomach tighten. He had survived his own brush with death through an extraordinary occurrence, but now…

Chunks fell into the river like siege stones hurled from catapults.

A heron soared across the trees, ignoring the activities below, diving after its silvery prey.

The bus moved another foot, sliding into the protective side wall, where massive cracks sprouted vein-like, spreading in all directions. An enormous section dropped out only yards from the stranded vehicle.

Lewis felt a tear on his cheek.

They would all be lost.

The men yelled, equally matching the frantic voices from within the bus, which grew even more hysterical if possible. Lewis felt a sharper stab of pain as he heard one of the men shout a name, over and over...

"Bobby, Bobby..."

It was the man's son. The boy was on the bus. *No!* They only had seconds left. The vehicle lurched to the side as the rest of the wall shattered. Nothing lay between the bus and oblivion now.

Lost.

Unless...

Could there be a way? Maybe there was. But he had to act *now*.

It took Lewis a fraction of a second to make the decision, and despite knowing that it would change his own life forever, it couldn't be helped. He would deal with the consequences. The cost was worth it. If there was a way to save the children, it didn't matter what else happened. He had survived when facing his own doom years past. These children must be given the same chance.

He had to at least try.

Lewis turned his head to the left, looking downstream. He angled his neck upwards, opened his mouth and spoke two words.

"Save them..."

Chapter Two

The bus slid toward the side, the front end already over the edge. It leaned downwards, and there was no chance of it stopping. Momentum and gravity were the masters here, and they would have their way.

The men shouted helplessly, already swimming to a point near where the bus would fall.

And fall it did.

Almost gracefully, the metal vehicle slanted at an increasingly sharper angle, until it was nosediving toward the river. There was nothing between it and the water. It fell half the distance, everything moving in slow motion now. Lewis felt himself go tense in anticipation.

The men were silenced by the anticipation of the tragedy to come, mouths opened in shock, eyes wide in terror.

A water heron looked up from the cattails, disturbed from its hunt.

And then the impossible happened...

The bus stopped in midair, hovering there only scant inches above the water.

The men were shocked, watching in disbelief. The whole world seem to shudder, then went still, all attention focused on this singular, fantastic, impossible event.

"Help them!"

It was Lewis who fractured the incredible moment, screaming over to the men, gesturing wildly with arms flailing.

Stunned, they swam closer towards the bus as the children continued to scream, some of their hands and faces visible from the inside. Several of them were already trying to climb through the windows. Within seconds, two of the men reached the vehicle, which seemingly defied gravity, floating steadily above the Sparse River, nothing beneath its bulk and the water but air itself. Children were now pouring out from the windows like frightened rats, and the men were hard-pressed to help them all. The other man came stumbling back from the road, and several onlookers from town now appeared, running to give aid. Lewis waded into the water, balancing himself against the steady current and heading for the mayhem. He helped a thin girl to the shore, gripping her shoulder tight and trying to soothe her cries. Things were happening so quickly, it was hard to keep an eye on all the children splashing in the river. If the current had been swifter, most of them would surely have drowned. Even now, there was no guarantee that all would be saved.

The seconds turned into minutes, and some of the men were now climbing into the bus, making sure that it was empty. The whole situation appeared outrageous, dream-like, but all actions were focused solely on getting the children to safety. The bus driver, Jack Reynolds, was one of the last ones out, and he helped a young boy climb through the emergency exit, finally exiting himself.

Most of them waded to the far side, which was closer to the suspended vehicle. Several of the men stood in the water, staring at the incredible vision of the bus which continued to hover there, defying logic and all the laws of physical science. It was a surrealistic scene, and all were swept up in something extraordinary.

"Everyone's out!" Someone yelled, and at the same moment one of the men screamed in horror, pointing at the windows. The sun was brilliant overhead, and the others looked to where he pointed. Without warning, the bus then shifted to the side, as if forced over by some great display of strength, then it hit the water with a thunderous splash, the bulk crawling downstream, slowed by its weight and lack of strong current, snagging on rocks and the bottom.

"Did you see it? Did you *see it?*"

The men backed away, moving toward the shore and as far away from the bus as possible, one of them falling forward, gasping for air. Their faces were ghastly pale, and one of them blessed himself.

Lewis felt his chest tighten at the sight, and he shook his head in shock.

"No," he whispered to himself. "Impossible."

Despite his own denial, he couldn't erase their reactions, and he could only draw one conclusion. They had *seen it!* He didn't know how, but their horror was unmistakable. He had wanted to save the children in the only way possible, regardless of how unbelievable it would look. He was the only one capable, their only hope. Even knowing that it would look miraculous, that perception would be infinitely better than the alternative…

Of someone actually seeing *what* had perpetrated the act.

Shaking himself, Lewis left the waters, looking around for more children, but a number of additional townsfolk had now arrived, and the situation appeared to be improving, although most of the kids were terrified, many crying. The children were safely on shore, and that was the important thing. They had been saved. Help continued to pour in from town. Police sirens screamed nearby, and the town fire station droned ominously in the distance, like a warning against danger from the skies.

Knowing it was time for him to slip away, Lewis grabbed his rod and vanished into the trees. The terrible event was over, and all attention would be focused on the safety of the children and returning them to their parents for now. The town would be in an uproar for days to come because of the bridge collapse, and the near disaster. And most certainly the fantastic way in which the children had been saved from death. Very soon, word would get out about what exactly these men had seen, and what his own role had been in all this. He couldn't change that fact. His presence had been noted, and fingers would be pointed. His only hope was that any conclusion, no matter how incredible, would keep him from being personally associated with the event.

Lewis didn't know what the fallout would be, but he knew one thing for certain.

It *would* come.

Chapter Three

The youth stared across the still waters of the pond, taking in the tranquil scene. A pair of swans glided by majestically, heads lifted proudly as they skirted the near edge. A large fish jumped from the middle, going airborne to pursue prey, its size and species unknown. Small fingerlings schooled together in the shallows, avoiding the deeper water and their cannibalistic brethren. A blue heron stood unmoving between lily pads, silent and methodical as it stalked its scaly meal.

He knew these things all had their place and purpose. Everything here was as natural as it could get. As it should be. Suddenly the heron dove its head into the water, pulling out a young bass which would not see its first full year of life. Watching this, he understood that even beneath the light of a warm, summer day, that *this picture of serenity held its dark side. The one which completed the full cycle of life and death. This revelation didn't make him sad, or even change his attitude at all. He merely accepted it as fact, what had always been, and what would always be.*

The swans came closer, several dozen yards away, and without warning they turned, heading for deeper waters. He wondered if they somehow sensed he was different, detected the presence of something unnatural, for that was the only explanation that described his existence.

Looking up, he spotted figures across the pond.

People from town, relaxing and enjoying the beautiful weather.

A couple walked together holding hands, laughing as one of their children galloped merrily after a large butterfly with a net. Feeling like an intruder, he watched as they stole a quick lover's kiss beneath the forlorn branches of a weeping willow tree. Several dozen yards from them sat a pair of young boys, talking and gesturing lazily as they kept a careful eye on their rods which were propped up on forked twigs, hoping for that telltale twitch which would indicate an interested visitor at the bottom of the pond.

Like the natural inhabitants of the environment, their human counterparts were a normal addition to the area, having carved out their unique and lasting niche.

The youth gazed at all this and felt a longing in his heart, realizing that he could never share this way of life. He was quietly growing into a young man, and was independent of anyone else. Fate had forced its iron hand upon him, leaving him no choice in the matter. There was nothing he could do to make things different. He didn't have the power to raise the dead, turn back the wheels of time and return his life to its former existence, simple as it had been. He couldn't undo the events which had made him into what he was.

But he still had feelings, longings.

There was a girl he liked in school, who had always treated him warmly. Someone who he connected with. If things were different, they might have grown together as a couple, been here even now like the others, walking across the grass, smiling and laughing, reveling in the pleasure of each other's company. A simple dream.

But no, it was not to be. Not now. Not ever.

This was something else in which he had no choice in the matter.

He stared into the woods behind him, although he didn't need his eyes to know the truth. There already existed a connection in his life, without any doubt. One that was powerful, unbreakable, and unfathomable. He had accepted this fact a while ago.

And knew that there wasn't a damn thing in all the world that could help him to change it...

Paul Melniczek

Chapter Four

"How are things going on in there?" Becky asked, peering around the corner to look at her cousin Samantha.

"All right, I guess." The young girl looked up, braids dangling across her shoulders as she paused with her stitching.

"Let me come and see. Lunch is almost done."

She walked into the living room where Samantha sat on the sofa facing the TV, both her lap and the coffee table littered with knitting patterns and material. The girl was working on a scene of a wooden covered bridge, brightly colored birds perched on the roof and a large sun in the background. It was a cheerful picture of tranquility, and Becky smiled. The look on her face was genuine, but inside her heart was heavy with worry.

"Wonderful, dear. I think you'll be able to win a

place at the fair this year."

"You really think so?"

"Yep." Becky tousled the girl's hair. "I know talent when I see it. And you've got it in bucket loads."

"Thanks." Samantha angled her head down shyly, resuming her work, while Becky backed off a pace, watching her. She was babysitting the girl on weekends as her aunt and uncle worked. They paid her enough, although truth be told, she would have done it for free because she loved the girl so much.

The girl she had nearly lost several days ago...

Becky shuddered, retreating into the kitchen. She couldn't get the vision out of her head, even though she hadn't actually witnessed it. The bridge collapsing, the children screaming in terror, the men watching helplessly from the riverside, waiting for the disaster to occur. In her nightmares, she had seen of all these things, waking up in the deep hours before dawn, a helpless witness to the impending tragedy, one which had been prevented by something which defied rational explanation.

As horrific as the accident had been, it paled in comparison to the talk about the event which had saved the lives of all the children, when the bus had stopped in midair, impossibly hovering over the cold waters below while the kids all fled to safety. There was not a single person in town unaffected by the extraordinary incident. Everywhere you went, people were discussing it. In the taverns, the shopping stores, at home and office, and in the church.

And the opinions varied drastically.

That is what Becky found to be the most disturbing. Especially the talk beginning to revolve around Lewis, and his possible hand in the entire episode. Fingers were being pointed more and more toward the strange and elusive young man, and not necessarily in a good way. Even her father had spoken of something extremely disquieting, concerning visions of something monstrous. Becky didn't believe in such talk, of course. If anything, she considered the whole affair nothing short of being miraculous. Why, all of the school children had been saved, including Samantha. A terrible disaster had been averted, a loss which would have scarred the small town for a generation to come, broken families, and ruined lives. It would have been something impossible to recover from.

But it had been prevented! They had all been saved!

Wasn't that good enough for some of the people? Well, it was, to some extent, at least. Attendance in the local churches had been at record levels lately. The pastors had heaped prayers of thanks for the outcome. Vigils were held, praising the heavens above that not a single child had been lost. But there were other rumblings spoken by others, some of the more extreme fundamentalists in town. Becky had not been there, but she'd heard enough of the gossip.

And she was very unnerved by all the rumors.

Snapping out of her reverie, she hurried to the oven and took out the brownies, which were slightly burned at the edges. She'd been careless, lost in thought.

Too much on my mind, she told herself. An image of Lewis then came into her head, and she paused, thinking of their friendship in school, only a few short years ago.

What had happened to them both since then? Well, she'd started working at the post office, and it looked good for her to work her way up in the next few years. She had a small circle of friends in the community, and spent free time with them. But there was certainly no romance in her life. She honestly could say there wasn't a single local boy she would even consider dating. The town was small, with not much to do besides work and drink at one of the several local watering holes. And unfortunately, that's where they all hung out, sitting next to their fathers and uncles as they came of age, and sometimes earlier, working at the same factory or occupation as they did, eventually morphing into a duplicate of their parents in the end. It was a future that Becky didn't want any part of, and she fully intended on building her job resume and leaving in a few short years. She couldn't do it just yet, but she was determined. And she was a pretty smart young girl, already with a decent job which could open up doors elsewhere.

And Lewis? What about him?

He lived on the mountain all alone, on a large property that he'd inherited in a tragic manner, a fire claiming the lives of his parents, the boy barely escaping with his own life. It had probably been the most terrible event ever in the community, and as a whole the people were a compassionate group, treating him with kindness and respect. He wasn't seen very often in town, but the citizens understood his aloofness.

He had been through a lot.

Becky fully understood all this, and had always been sympathetic. They were friends in school, close friends, and she missed his companionship. There had been glimmers of something beyond a casual relationship between the two, but it had never reached its potential. Lewis had always managed to keep himself a safe distance away from her each time they seemed to be getting closer. It had been a frustrating period of time, and Becky had been hurt. He'd never mistreated her in any way except by his inaction, but that had been enough. She forgave him though, and still cared for him. After all, you couldn't force a relationship, no less love, on another person.

The Unseen

So when all this talk started revolving more and more around Lewis, Becky began to feel disturbed, increasingly worried where it all might lead. Something incredible had happened in their small town, an event which people were trying to understand and deal with. There was no precedent for this incident, nothing which offered up any background for explanation, and Becky understood how the hearts and minds of people operated as well as anyone else.

Ignorance of the unknown could lead to widespread speculation, even fear.

And where fear existed, action might also follow, however misguided.

Paul Melniczek

Chapter Five

Lewis sat on his wooden front porch and stared over the top of the forest which encircled the valley, the ground sloping gradually downwards until it reached town far below, which was hidden behind the wall of trees and a flow of gradually curving hills. A bluebird chirped from a dogwood tree, flapping its wings. A pair of rabbits chased each other across the meadow, engaged in springtime courtship, scattering a pair of brightly-hued butterflies which fluttered gracefully away. It looked to be a pleasant day, but other things weighed heavily over him, and the activities surrounding him were only small distractions.

Lewis watched the playful creatures without really seeing them, deep in thought. He rocked gently back and forth, chewing on a long piece of grass, still moist from dew. He took it slowly from his mouth, then

Paul Melniczek

placed it in again, the act absently indecisive. Several days had now passed since the incident at the bridge, and he'd stayed at home the entire time, sequestered up on his land in the hills. The property was very secluded. No other roads went past his own driveway, and the nearest neighbor lived two miles away. Behind him was a large wilderness of state-owned land, most of it purchased from the company which had once scavenged the hills and woods in a thirsty quest for coal.

Some said that the spirits of lost miners still walked among the abandoned shafts and mines, restless, in a search for final peace. Lewis regarded the idea with an open mind, and believed they remained connected to the place of their demise. It was difficult to deny such tales, based on the irrationality of his own existence.

Eyes closed, he lifting his head, sensing without looking, searching out the presence of another. Dropping his chin back down, he shook his head, wondering for the millionth time what it all meant. This area was a fitting home for him, and he understood that it was better this way. Here, no one bothered him, and he lived in his own world. It was a frontier of sorts, and he looked at himself as being verged on two borders; one of the real world, and the other...something completely different. Whether he cared for such arrangements really wasn't the question, and would solve nothing. He was a very unique person. He was pretty sure, no, convinced -- that no one else in all the waking world shared his particular problem...if that was the proper term. Words to describe his situation were inadequate. Everything fell far short. Logic, words, theories.

Hopes. Dreams.

The only thing he knew for *certain* was the reality of his situation -- the undeniable truth, and there was nothing to be done about it.

He looked over to the left side of his house to see

where his companion now was, his neck craning upwards. Yes, it was there waiting, of course. As always. No matter the time of day or night, season of the year, it was there. Regardless of his mood, state of mind, emotional standing, it remained nearby. Lewis turned away, his face expressionless. Nothing registered except a pale glimmer of recognition deep within his orbs. All other reactions were ghosts of the past, now faded into oblivion. If anyone else would have seen through his eyes, though, even for a fraction of a second, they would have been shocked, horrified beyond belief.

But not him. Not anymore, at least. The years had brought about a grudging acceptance.

An understanding? Absolutely not. Never.

At best it was a coming to terms with his own life, and the extraordinary details of it. On the surface Lewis appeared very mundane. Average, likable, but otherwise pretty much unremarkable. On the *surface*.

But go deeper?

Oh, no...

Paul Melniczek

Chapter Six

The four men huddled together in *Dog's Tavern,* each of them with beer mugs either in hand or on the wooden table, several shot glasses scattered about, all of them empty. The room was smoky and dark, and other customers sat or milled about, pecking away in conversation. Two men in their early twenties were shooting a game of pool, now eyeing up a tough break. The waitress, a bleached blond with a cigarette hanging from her lip, routinely went about picking up empty glasses, moving in such fashion that she appeared almost mechanical. Mike Evans, the owner and part-time mixologist, leaned against a paneled support pillar from behind the L-shaped bar, watching the television mounted to the wall and chatting with several men on stools, regulars to the last one, all of them firmly in the grips of various hard liquors.

Pete West brought the beer to his mouth at the table of four, his hand trembling. "I swear I'll never frickin' sleep again." He kept shaking his head, back and forth, his gaze focused elsewhere -- a place dark and horrible. The others looked around, none of them willing to stare into each others' eyes.

"We all saw it. Nothing we could have imagined separately." Jack Reynalds smashed a cigar into an ashtray, his meaty fingers twisting it around in lazy circles. He slumped back into his chair, rubbing his forehead. "I still can't believe it. What the hell was it?"

"I don't *want* to know what it was!" Parker, the youngest of the group by a dozen years, made a fist, grinding it into the table. His hair was down to his shoulders, coal-black, and his eyes held a haunted look, dark circles smudging the skin beneath them. "I told Nancy that I want to move, get a thousand miles away from here and never look back!"

Pete nodded, the heavy man perspiring, his face flushed. "I don't blame you for wanting that. Things will never be the same here."

The fourth man, Grant, the plant manager at the hat factory, was silent. He was the oldest, his hair flecked with gray, his face deeply wrinkled. "A bunch of others from town saw the bus, or else they'd have called us all liars. I would have too, by hell…But we ain't liars. We saw what we *saw*. The last one of us here will swear on a stack of all the holy books in the world that it's all true." He stared them down. "Anyone care to disagree?"

An uncomfortable silence, fidgeting under the table, hands moving awkwardly.

Grant continued, waving the waitress over for another round of shots and drinks. He lowered his voice. "There's more to it. I think that *thing* we saw is up there in the mountain, is associated with Lewis."

"Don't even talk about it." Parker said, his voice

quivering. "I'm scared to death already."

"We *have* to talk about it." Grant said.

"But what *was* it?" Jack shuffled nervously in his chair.

"How the hell should I know?" Grant snapped at him. "It wasn't anything meant to be in this world, that's for damn sure." He paused for a long moment. "It's something evil. A monster, or maybe even a demon."

None of them rebuked his statement. All of them believed him. But Pete shook his head. "But it stopped the bus from falling. Why did it save the kids then? Answer me that."

"I don't know why...Evil works in strange ways. In whatever fashion it sees fit." Grant leaned forward, his voice faltering. "But nothing *good* can come of it. Something bad's gonna' happen because of that thing. Real bad. I never thought I'd see anything that would make me know the devil was with us. But he *is*, right here in our little town. And Lewis controls it, or something like that. It has to be. Demons are real -- we've seen the truth with our own eyes."

Parker agreed. "He told us to help them, like it was nothing for a bus to float in the air. And then he left after the kids were all on shore and safe. Nobody's seen him since."

Grant gestured with his thumb. "That's why he stays all alone up there on the ridge. Living with that...horrible thing." He shuddered, chills crawling along his back. The others shook their heads, and Jack winced, all of them terrified to the man. "It all makes sense now."

The waitress came over, and Grant signaled for another round of drinks to follow, slapping a twenty in her hand. When she left, he spoke again. "We have to do something about it. Before it's too late."

"What do you mean?" Parker's eyes were wide,

and they all stared at Grant, horror etched into their faces.

"We'll take care of Lewis."

"Are you out of your mind?" Parker rose from his chair. "With that monster living up there? No way, not for all the money in the world..." Pete swore, and Jack's knee bumped the table.

"Shut up and sit down, you fool. Listen to me, all of you." He waited a moment for them to settle before continuing again. "You're forgetting something important here." Grant's voice was icy, and he stared at them all in turn. "Ain't none of you going to like this one damn bit, but you have to listen, and understand. We all saw it, the four of us. Right?"

They were silent to the man, listening to his terrible words.

"We *saw it.*"

Parker's mouth hung open, and his left eye twitched. "Yeah," he answered. "We all agree on that one, so help me."

"All right. Now here's the thing. All of us here saw that creature. So what do you think that means? Think!" Grant swore under his breath, shaking his head before continuing. "It *knows* we saw it, knows about us."

"How do you figure that?" Pete asked.

"By our reactions! Our faces. How else? Now back to what I was saying...What does this mean?"

But none of them had an answer, and he was greeted only with looks of shock and confusion. The waitress returned with the bottle, refilling all their empties. The men said nothing as she dropped their change, seemingly disinterested in anything else but moving on to the next table and its waiting drinkers.

She left, and after a moment Grant shook his head in disbelief. "Are you all blind and deaf? Don't any

42

of you understand what I'm even talking about here? The consequences of our knowledge? I can't be the only one who figured this out." He paused for a moment. "All right. Listen to me, and listen real close. Our lives depend on it, I tell you. Yours, and mine. Because how long do you think it will be until that thing comes down from the hills and comes after *us*?"

There was nothing else he could have said which would have frightened them more. Parker's face melted into a deeper shade of pale. Pete's breathing was harsh, and he sounded on the verge of an asthma attack. Jack looked as if someone had just knifed him in the back. A man at the bar shouted at something on TV, and Parker knocked over his mug of beer, ignoring the liquid forming a small wake in front of him. They were all ghouls, their faces hellish to look at.

But Grant's expression was the worse. His eyes were wild with fear -- and passion.

"That *thing* will come hunting us all. You think it will let us go for long, knowing what we know? It's waiting now, I tell you. Waiting for the right time to find and hunt us down." He nodded his head slowly. "Waiting, for now. But it'll come looking for us, sooner...or later. And when it does..."

He didn't need to finish, his words having the desired effect on his companions.

The candle in the center of the table flickered ominously, and they sat there in silence, their terror almost a living thing, growing in strength, devouring their confidence, shaking them to their very souls, clouding all other thought. And within their minds, unbidden, formed a shared vision of what they'd seen reflected in the windows of the bus -- the terrible creature which could only have been spawned in nightmare, emerging from some blackened pit far removed from everything they knew and understood.

Paul Melniczek

"I have to go," said Grant, downing his shot and standing. "But we'll talk again tomorrow. I want all of you here, same time. Got it?"

He left the silent table, and the rest of them huddled just a bit closer together, a subconscious act of primeval fear.

The ghouls would have no sleep that night, and perhaps never again.

Chapter Seven

Becky walked through the kitchen, pulling her night robe tightly about her. Bedtime hunger cravings were her weakness, no doubt.

How would she ever lose that last ten pounds if she kept snacking every night?

Sighing, she opened the cabinet above the oven, pausing as she heard voices in the living room. Hmm, her parents were up a bit later than usual, she thought. She stopped, hoping it wasn't an argument. Although they rarely argued, things had been difficult the past few days, ever since the accident with the school bus. The town was ablaze with rumors and strange stories, and it bothered her a lot. Especially all the talk about Lewis and his involvement in some way. Gossip resounded off the walls of their small town, snaking its insidious way into each and every household. Theirs was no exception.

She listened as her father, Grant, spoke with her mother, his voice taking on a harsh tone, nearly hysterical.

"It has to be done…You didn't see it, but others saw what happened to the bus. My men from the plant. You think we're all just lying, making this up? How else can you explain to me what happened then?"

Her mother was silent, but Becky could picture her face when she was under stress. The pinched lip, the blinking eyes, the hands clenched at her sides. She was certain that was exactly how she would appear now, if Becky were to make an impromptu entrance into the next room. But that was not going to happen.

"Lewis…it ain't natural, he's not human. A freak. Living with that thing up there. It's the devil, I say. Who knows what it will do next."

"I don't know what to think. I wasn't there, but it all sounds so…unbelievable." Her mother's voice was low, uncertain.

"It *is* unbelievable. How do you think I felt when I saw it? When we all saw it? Anyone ever tell me such a thing I would call them a fool or drunk, or both. But it's *me* talking here. I'm the one who experienced it, although I don't know why I was chosen."

"Even though all the children were saved? You think it has something to do with…" She paused, unwilling to go further. Becky's mother was very religious, and also superstitious. And she preferred sweeping unpleasant things beneath the carpet, living by the motto 'out of sight, out of mind'.

But her husband was of a different breed, and would have none of it. Especially in his own home.

"Yes. I do. It's a demon, I tell you. Something monstrous, not from *here*. And for whatever reason it saved the kids. For now. It's after something more than lives, you hear me. Something more precious."

The Unseen

"Please, don't say anymore." Voice shaking, the woman pleaded with her husband.

The voices were quiet for long moments and Becky held her breath, the house seeming to hunker down about them, the shadows in the corners menacing, concealing secrets. Her skin grew cold as she replayed her father's words about Lewis. *Freak, not human.* She'd heard her father's original description about what happened shortly after the incident, although Grant had told her to say nothing to anyone else. But she didn't believe his explanation. It was impossible. They had imagined something, all of them. There had to be something that was missing, a piece of the puzzle that had been overlooked. Maybe some naturally occurring phenomenon, having to do with air currents and temperature. Multiple people had seen the bus hovering above the river, so the event wasn't in doubt. But the rationalization of the event had been horribly twisted, leading to an ominous conclusion. Superstition was now clouding their judgment, her father not the least.

"Something's got to be done, before it comes looking for us."

Becky felt her chest go numb, and the implications of what her father argued frightened her.

What was he talking about? He thought they might be in danger? Was he going mad?

This was too much for her. She had known Lewis for years, and they'd gone to school together. He was harmless, if shy. She couldn't believe he was in league with the devil...or anything else.

And monsters? She shook her head. *It was crazy, the whole idea was ridiculous. But her father sounded serious -- deadly serious.*

She tiptoed away, leaving through the other doorway, heading for the stairs. The quiet town had transformed into something else since the accident at the bridge. It had changed, and not for the better. The children had been saved, but that fact seemed to have been swept away, replaced by something far more sinister. She had the feeling that something terrible was going to happen, and it wasn't difficult to follow the eventual destination as to where this road would lead to...

Lewis.

She needed to take action. By herself. And soon. She knew her father very well, and he was not someone who could be shaken from what he believed in, once convinced. It was simply not in his blood. And he was very influential in the community. Plant manager, and president of the church council. A formidable adversary, if one were to cross him. Even a family member.

Oh, this was awful. How could she persuade her father that he was making a terrible mistake, casting such dreadful accusations on someone who was completely innocent, and incapable of harming another?

The answer was an easy one. She would be unable to sway him. She could beg, argue, get down on her hands and knees, but the depth of Grant's convictions, once reached, eliminated any possible change of heart. The man was her father, and she loved him dearly, but she also knew how inflexible he was.

Becky quietly entered her bedroom, her appetite now extinguished and replaced by a knot of anxiety, tossing and turning, roiling about like a disturbed tomcat. Sweat beaded upon her brow, and a chill worked its slow way beneath her robe.

What in the world was she going to do?

Chapter Eight

Lewis felt troubled. He frowned, thinking about the recent events. He hadn't asked for any of this...Not the way his life had evolved, what it had evolved *into*. He was an outsider, would always be an outsider. That couldn't be altered. And he'd accepted it fully. But now, other things had changed drastically. People had seen the impossible way the bus had been prevented from crashing, and the whole town was shocked. He didn't need to be out in the streets, talking, or listening to their conversations.

He knew better. And how long would it be until he was implicated with the events? Lewis could have denied any hand in it, if only the men hadn't seen.

If only...

But they *had* seen, oh yes...although he didn't know how this had happened. A brief glimpse, a chance reflection from the sun against the windows, maybe. A unique circumstance of sort. That was all that was needed. Small in itself, but enough for a lasting, haunting impression. Lewis had always wondered if anyone else would ever see what he did. He'd assumed that it couldn't happen, never in his lifetime, but the freak accident had proven otherwise. In the past, it had traveled alongside him, unseen, unnoticed, by any but himself. It was the most bizarre thing anyone could have imagined. His invisible companion, constantly with him.

So the question remained, what would those men do?

It was an ugly thought, but also an unavoidable one as well. Lewis needed to think things through. When placed in extraordinary situations, especially those based in fear, people reacted. And many times with drastic outcomes. *This* qualified. This was most certainly something beyond their comprehension. It was beyond *his* comprehension. So there it was. The dice had been rolled, fate had chosen its main characters, and now they were all swept up in it. At least to some capacity. Would the townspeople actually do something? Or maybe do nothing at all, and let him live his life by himself as an outsider, afraid to antagonize him? That would be the best possible course for them to take. And he believed the majority of people would follow suit. But there lurked the possibility that some would disagree, maybe even try to drive him away.

And if they did?

What would *he* do about it? The last thing he wanted was for anyone to get hurt. But this wasn't necessarily within his control, and if someone approached him with bad intentions, there *would* be retribution.

Not from him though...

Lewis walked through the house, his hand idly

skimming against the walls, feeling the old wallpaper. The place was quiet, but not empty. Lewis was never really alone, had not been alone for long years. He constantly wished things were different, but all the wishing in the world couldn't change that fact. Restless, he wandered to the front porch, slumping into the rocking chair. This was his spot. It was here that he was most comfortable, where he could look out upon the valley at his feet, and try to make sense of things. Over the years, he'd certainly contemplated much from his vantage point in the hills, sequestered away from the small artery of civilization below. Long hours sitting and thinking, and always coming up empty, without any answers, only more questions. An endless cycle with no breakage in sight.

And now, once more, he really needed to try to sort things out.

It was a terrible misfortune that fate had placed upon him with recent events. But he couldn't have stood by and let the children fall to their almost certain death. It was unthinkable. He was not that type of person, never had been. Never would be. And in this unforeseen way, his unique situation had done something which brought about an act of good. Lives were saved, and parents basked in the blessing which enabled the rescue of their sons and daughters. There was no questioning the fruits of his decision.

Tragedy had been averted.

But it wasn't the end of the matter. If it were all just about the results, then this would be over by now, and everyone could return to their former lives, however mundane or extraordinary. Unfortunately, it was the *manner* of this action which had changed everything...The bus, hovering in air without any possible explanation, and several men catching a glimpse of what had stopped it.

In years past, he would have been drowned in water, buried under stone, or even burned at the stake, for participating, or causing, something which could only be construed as an act of witchery and black magic.

And was this very far from the truth?

No, it wasn't.

He felt a chill crawl along his spine. Yes, he had much in common with those folks who had suffered in the past. They were his fallen brethren, persecuted for their actions, real or not. He could almost feel their presence nearby, invisibly surrounding him, eyes staring wide in recognition at his own fate.

But there was no time to dwell on speculation from a historical basis.

The intervention *had* occurred, and could not be undone, despite all the misgivings and wishing he could muster. Lewis had chosen to act, bringing about the means to save the children. And this intervention surely made him the perpetrator of the incredible action. Without question. Despite the enlightenment of this supposedly openminded age, there still were many things beyond the understanding of men. Things which were best left alone, untouched, unapproached. Truths which lurked in the twilight of this world, waiting patiently on the fringe of reality for their particular moment of revelation. Science and logic were useless here, effectless to answer any questions. For there was no valid explanation to resolve the circumstances. Lewis himself was at a loss to comprehend his own situation, and he lacked the slightest understanding of the thing which warded over him…

His invisible keeper, his protector.

Chapter Nine

Grant stood outside on the sidewalk letting the cool air wash against his face, enjoying the brief comfort of relief from the inner fire that simmered deep within his chest. The sky was clear overhead, pinpricks of starlight piercing the canopy of black. It was a pleasant spring evening, nigh on summer which would arrive within days.

Looking up at the steeple, Grant's eyes were intense, twin cinders of tiny flame. Stalking away, he mumbled to himself, a struggle waging inside his large frame. He knew what needed to be done, but he was afraid. Terrified to death, of both acting out *and* holding back. The consequences of either one weighed on him like a physical burden.

"Give me strength. Give me the courage to do what needs to be done." He stared skywards, whispering to himself. Shivering, he knew that the chill he felt wasn't from the air.

The men were frightened to the bone. That was obvious. Hell, wasn't he? Without question. But he couldn't let the *others* see that. If they doubted his resoluteness, even for a single moment, their chance would be lost. Oh yes, he was mighty scared indeed. He'd always believed in the existence of evil things in the world. There had to be, balanced by all that was good, and he was a firm convert to this line of thought, the order to which he went about living his life. It was the way of the universe, the way it was meant to be.

Good and evil. Proper and natural.

But he never thought that he would actually *see* the truth before his own eyes, materializing in such a profound and heinous way…

Grant shuddered, banishing a monstrous vision of the terrible creature. *Lewis was the key.* There was no doubt of this in his mind. He would stake his life on that if needed.

He was connected to that thing.

Isolated, Lewis was a self-imposed outcast, living on the far reaches of their community way up on the forested ridge, part of a chain of foothills that bulged throughout the region. All the signs were there, but no one had ever questioned his motivation before. In reality, there had been no reason to question his isolation before this event. Orphaned, Lewis had inherited the property from his dead parents after the fire had consumed everything, and life had gone on for the boy since that time. The townsfolk had reached out in compassion, hoping he would come out fine in the end. It had been his choice to remain aloof, but that was understandable.

Grant paused, leaning against a brick wall. *Yes, he understood perfectly now. Well, almost.* He didn't know exactly what Lewis was, or the monster. Part of him was curious to know. That road was perilous, but his mind couldn't stay away from that dark little corner which searched for answers, however terrible. Once, when Grant had been a child, a wake had been held in his house. He'd been told of the tradition, and who was at rest in the casket. Told not to worry, the event would be over soon. It was normal, nothing to fear. And later that night, he'd wandered downstairs on his own, tip-toeing into the living room, moving steadily nearer to the ominous black box which housed his dead relative inside, his heart beating loudly enough that he thought his parents *must* hear, his hands reaching to the edge…

Grant pushed himself away from the wall, expelling the disturbing memory. No, he didn't want to remember the face that had stared back at him that night…lifeless, chalky white. He wondered if this was how his own face must look right now. Pale and drained of life.

He stalked the streets for a while, a wandering ghoul, his head flooded with a vortex of emotions and ideas, theories and plans, hopes and fears. He was in many ways the leader of the town, and people looked to him for answers. He must not falter in his determination. Something monstrous lurked nearby, its purpose unknown, its very nature unknown. Something which should not exist, but did.

And his tormented mind continued to pursue avenues of thought on what exactly needed to be done. It would be a long night for him.

Paul Melniczek

Chapter Ten

He ran through the woods, whipping past low-lying tree branches which snatched at his jacket. Leaves scattered in his passing, recently fallen as autumn claimed the surrounding countryside, painting it in hues of burnt orange and faded yellow. Slipping on mossy rocks, he angled his head behind him, frantically searching for any sign of pursuit.

There was nothing there.

His chest heaving from the exertion, he continued pumping his legs, trying to ignore the tightness in his hamstrings and the cramps in his chest. He willed his body onwards, not daring to stop. He was in a race, but it was by himself. Sweat beaded on his brow, and he licked the saltiness from his lips. The air was cool, but he felt the shirt clinging uncomfortably to his back with clammy hands. Once he stumbled and fell to his knees, but he pushed himself up immediately, finding hidden reserves of strength which propelled him ahead.

And away from the thing that might be following...

It was getting dark out, and a premature nightfall was blanketing the landscape with dusky shadows. Overhead, tree boughs took on a menacing form, trembling in the wind, clutching blindly at the air like crooked fingertips. A rotten trunk lay in his path, and he hurdled it, dropping smoothly onto the other side and never missing a step. He was athletic, hardened by living on the mountain, and learning to fend for himself. All he wanted was to be left alone and lead a simple life.

But fate had other plans in store for him.

His mind drifting, he nearly went over the edge of a ridge which suddenly loomed before him from out of nowhere. Waving his arms, he steadied himself, finding his balance. To either side the edge continued, rocky and treacherous, the forest serving as barrier against the slope below. This was new territory for him, and he'd never been here before, bursting through the woods and running for all that he was worth.

What now?

Gritting his teeth, he bent forward, catching his breath for a moment, but he refused to stop here. He needed to make a decision, and it only took a second for him to choose. He wanted nothing to do with the dark woods behind him, and what lurked there, somewhere unseen. So he braced himself, plunging down over the edge, half-sliding, half-pawing at the shale and loose rock, desperately trying to stay on his feet and avoid tumbling headlong to the bottom, which appeared to be a long way off. It was steep enough that he would be seriously hurt, if not killed, if he fell.

He considered this for a moment, but then

realized that his life -- any life -- was too precious to waste, regardless of the challenges.

And his challenge was mighty indeed.

Disturbing the slope, his descent was difficult, his movement creating mini-landslides which threatened to undermine the entire section in which he maneuvered. It took everything he had to keep from losing control and spinning helplessly downwards. His mind was now entirely focused on his actions, and he momentarily forgot what he was even running from, caught up in the exhilaration of the dangerous climb. Over halfway down, his left foot caught on a snag, and he felt himself go face forward, arms swinging to his front in an attempt to avoid injury. He landed on his stomach, and now was sliding down, headfirst. Panicking, he reached out with one arm and grabbed onto a cluster of rocks which were deeply embedded into the hillside. He managed to slow down, and then righted himself, sporting several new bruises and cuts, but nothing serious. He made good time, and the bottom was drawing near.

Steady, he told himself. You're almost there.

Long seconds later he reached the base of the slope, and raced forward, determined to put the obstacle behind him.

And between himself and what was surely following.

The forest continued, the geography appearing much the same as before. He had no real plan, just a spontaneous impulse to escape the madness of his life, hoping that his actions would change things, show his resoluteness.

Hurtling through the eaves of the wood, he ran for another minute, finding his way blocked again, this time by a small river. He knew the water would be cold, but without hesitation he entered, fervently wishing that it would confuse the trail, throw off his scent, or whatever it was that linked him to his pursuer. But he wasn't going to deceive himself, for he realized that it might be something else entirely which was at play here; some form of connection which was beyond his comprehension. When it came to the details of his life, anything was possible, he'd come to believe.

And not least of all the impossible...

The current was moderate, and he had little trouble negotiating it. At one point he looked over his shoulder, and saw nothing. Felt nothing as well. For he'd come to recognize the presence of his unwanted companion, and could always feel the closeness of its proximity.

He didn't feel it right now, but he didn't want to jump ahead to any conclusions, however hopeful or false.

Reaching the middle, the waters pulled him downstream and he was soaked to the skin, but he didn't care. Shortly he gained the other side, which was only a leveling of the landscape, a mixture of rounded river stones and packed mud. Overhead, the early evening stars glittered, and he glanced up for a second, wondering if that's where it came from. A billion miles away, or perhaps some other dimension.

Wherever the origin, it was not from here, he knew.

More trees surrounded him, and he pushed himself between the closest trunks, knowing that he was growing weary, and would be unable to keep this up for too much longer. Maybe there would be a road ahead somewhere, or a cabin. He'd left his home in a rush, having reached the breaking point.

Run or go entirely mad. It had been that simple. It was a wonder that he still retained all his mental faculties, living his life this way since his parents had *died. He still cried at times, missing them dearly, hating the cruel act which had swept them away, and made his life into the hell that it now was. The unbelievable, undeniable, irrationality of his daily existence, which defied all explanation.*

He felt ready to collapse, still moving forward, unwilling, maybe unable to stop. He wondered if this would be his fate, running heedlessly ahead until he fell and broke his neck, putting an end to it all for good.

And then he had a horrifying thought, stopping him literally in his tracks… What if his fate superceded even the boundary between life and death?

Terrified by the notion, he heard low growling from ahead, and to his left side.

He had other things to worry about now, as a pair of dogs emerged, one of them black and gray, teeth bared, mouth foaming as it showed its maw. Another one trotted from the bushes to the side, smaller, but looking just as unpleasant.

Packs of wild dogs frequented the area, as everyone knew. Some had escaped from abusive households, others from illegal fighting kennels, and there were even some renegades once used to guard stills. They all had a nasty background, and roamed the countryside, taking down deer and anything else they could find. There had been a few attacks on people, although rare.

And it looked like he was about to become a candidate for that low percentage…

Weaponless, he bent down and picked up a branch, trying to remember the best plan of engagement when facing a wild animal. There was something he recalled about staring it in the eyes, but he didn't remember whether it was to do so, or avoid it, but he never had the chance as the dogs crouched down with hairs raised, their ears flattening. Something huge erupted from the tree line behind him, and the first dog was snatched off its feet, flying through the air in a show of tremendous power. It crashed into a solid oak tree directly behind it, flung end over end before falling in the brush. The second dog didn't have time to even react, as it was picked up and thrown dozens of yards into the gloom, yelping once before falling silent.

He was stunned by the savagery of the action and stood there, shaking from the cold and fear, the branch hanging limply in his hand, then dropping softly to the ground. His keeper loomed before him, quiet and unmoving once more, now that the threat had been vanquished.

He was horrified on multiple levels, and tried to find his way to clarity, regain some sense of calm to put things into perspective. His heart sank, knowing that escape was impossible, as the thing would pursue him relentlessly no matter where he went. There were no frontiers that could hide him, no walls which would sequester him away from his fate. The creature was the perfect protector, making sure he was kept safe. It was also the ultimate predator, able to move silently and invisibly wherever it deemed necessary. And the power it possessed...

He had known all along that it was strong, based solely on its sheer size and mass. In hand-to-hand combat, certainly nothing on the planet could match its ferocity. It was a killing machine, pure and simple. Efficient and ruthless. Unforgiving, uncompromising.

And it was his protector, his guardian against anything which threatened. To wield the ability to enact such devastation was overwhelming. He had no idea of his control over the creature, if he really had any, but he swore to himself then, vowing never to command it for anything destructive. The potential was unlimited.

Staggered by the thought, he slumped to the cool

earth, watching his monstrous companion for some movement, a sign or signal, anything that would relay its real motivation. It was obvious that it would fend him from harm, but still gave no indication as to why it did so.

He looked up at it, gazing into those terrible orbs, which blazed with an inner fire -- a mixture of intelligence, rage, and purpose, all combined into a life form which defied all knowledge and reason.

"Why me?" He asked. "What do you want with me? Where did you come from? Why are you protecting me?"

He was greeted by silence. He might as well have been talking with the mountains, asking them what the meaning of life was.

"I know you understand me. Communicate with me, give me a sign, please. I can't stand going on like this. Don't you see? I'm grateful for what you've done, but you can go away now, go back to wherever you came from. I don't want you here..."

His voice trailed off, and he crumbled to the ground, overcome by fatigue, the cold, and his injuries.

And then, like a mother handling its cub, the creature bent down, picking him up effortlessly and carrying him away through the night, retracing the way they had come.

Paul Melniczek

Chapter Eleven

The road climbed steadily upwards, and Becky leaned forward in her seat nervously. She knew where Lewis lived, although she'd never been to his house before. He lived alone, ever since the death of his parents many years ago, but little else did she know about him. Just memories from school, friends who enjoyed each other's company, although she had been trying to become closer to him. Students were grouped alphabetically, and their last names were similar, ensuring them years of mutual classes together. She figured that he lived off the inheritance left from his deceased parents, and it must have been sizable enough for him not to work, unless he practiced an occupation which didn't require access to the town. She really didn't know.

Trees connected overhead, the forest looking old

and watchful. The woods were dense, and bushes surrounded the wide trunks, scraping for every possible inch of purchase, battling against creepers and long vines. The whole area appeared unpleasant, stifling. It was a natural barrier from town and the outlying houses. To her, it was unknown territory. She swallowed heavily.

Without warning, the trees broke open, and a wide green meadow spread out before her, the grass a vibrant green from the pleasant spring weather they were experiencing.

The house was in view.

Nothing spectacular, just a decent-sized country log home, picturesque as it sat at the foot of the hillcrest behind. The woods ended sharply, beginning again behind the structure where it became a black thicket, guarding the high places. She slowed her sedan, spotting Lewis immediately, standing at the foot of the porch, hands on hip, as if expecting her. Stopping the vehicle, she opened the door and stepped out. The sky had clouded over, and the air felt cooler than at her home. Elevation made a difference. She was struck by the isolation up here. It was nothing compared to the dusty old town, but here beneath the open sky and with the woods now behind her, she actually liked it.

"Hi, Lewis. How are you?"

He held his ground, his face showing his surprise. "Becky? It *is* you...What are you doing here?"

"That's hardly a warm welcome, don't you think?" She came forward until they were only separated by a few feet. "It's kinda' nice up here, away from it all. Seems that's the way you prefer it, I guess."

Lewis narrowed his eyes, the only visible sign that he was nervous himself. Becky noticed it immediately. "I'll get right to it, then. I think you're in danger."

"What are you talking about?"

"There's a lot of talk going around town about the accident with the bus. They're saying terrible things about you. I'm afraid...something might happen."

Lewis made no expression, but Becky thought that there was a hint of sadness, deep within his orbs. His brown hair hung limply, and he hadn't shaved in several days. The stain of dark circles began to show beneath his eyes. He didn't answer her, but his face saddened even more, and he looked past her, toward the town. "Is that why you came here then?"

"Why, yes. What do you mean by that?"

He hesitated. "I know all about the stories they're telling. You've heard them by now."

"I have."

"And?"

"And what?"

Lewis stared hard at her. "Whatever they're saying, do you believe them?"

Becky now looked surprised. "Of course not."

"Then what do *you* think happened to save the children?"

She was silent for long moments. The sky clouded more, and she felt an uncomfortable chill. Maybe it wasn't as nice up here as she had previously thought...

Lewis spoke before she could answer. "It was something incredible which happened. You came here to warn me, but also for another reason. To convince yourself that I had nothing to do with it. And...I'm really glad to see you again."

She blushed. "Me too. It's been a while, Lewis."

There was an uncomfortable pause, then Becky continued. "But I'm serious about what I said, Lewis. My father thinks that you're hiding something bad. I *don't* believe that. I know who you are."

They stared at each other, and Becky was shocked by his response. "But I *did* have something to do with it, Becky." His voice was so low that she barely caught the words. She didn't know what to think. "And they must *not* come here for any reason."

"Are you saying...that you'll hurt them?" She was stunned.

"No! Never. Not me. I can't explain, and I don't want to tell you more than I have already. Some things are out of my control, that's the best way I can describe it." He lifted his hands for emphasis, but the gesture fell short, as words and motions both seemed inadequate. "I've never told anyone even this much -- and I'm sorry. Really, truly sorry. But you have to tell them not to come up here."

"They'll never believe me...And you know my father. If he even suspects that I came to see you, he'll march right up here with a lynch mob."

Lewis closed his eyes, looking pained, then turned his head to the left, lifting it a bit, and staring. Becky followed his gaze, but there was nothing there. And for some reason, she found his odd posture very disturbing. Lewis moved back, sinking onto the bottom step leading up to the porch. "They can't come here. If they try to harm me..." He didn't finish.

Becky was confused, and worried. She knelt down, facing him, trying desperately to make sense of it all. "Please tell me what's wrong. You can trust me."

Lewis nodded, his face sad. "You're probably the only person I could actually trust. But I won't. I can't bring you into this any further. No..."

"They won't let it rest," she said. "I overheard my parents talking last night. He's going to do something, probably soon. Maybe bring some men up here and talk with you, or even the sheriff. Lewis, I want to help, but you're not letting me." She paused. "You've never given me a chance, you know."

He sighed. "I remember back in school, you were always friendly to me. I never fit in, but it didn't matter to you at all. I...I liked what we had." Lewis smiled -- a warm, genuine expression, which looked good on him.

Becky smiled in return. "So *tell* me what to do then. I swear I'll help you, no matter what."

Lewis hesitated, clearly struggling with his next words. He put his face into his hands and rubbed his eyes. "I don't know. I'll leave, maybe. That's the only way to make sure people don't get hurt."

"I can't begin to understand anything you're talking about," Becky said. "If they come here and try to take you away, or hurt you, then you'll defend yourself? But you won't go after them? Lewis, help me here...I don't understand what you're talking about."

"No, you don't. And nothing will ever happen to them in town, I swear to you. It's just that they *can't* try to come after me. Not here, not anywhere. Something terrible would happen. I know you're confused, but there's no other way to tell you this. Just take my word, trust *me* now. You always believed in me before." He paused, his voice husky. "Becky, I can't thank you enough for all the kindness you've shown me in the past. And if things had been different..." He drifted off uncertainly. "But you *have* to leave. And please don't come here again. For your own sake."

With that, he turned and went inside, never looking back.

She was more confused than ever. Nothing he said made any sense at all. She was hurt, frightened for him -- and for her father as well. The stubborn man would stop at nothing once his mind was set. No argument in the world could turn him. She'd come here to find some type of resolution to the growing problem.

Instead, she had found only more questions, and little hope. There were questions that were unanswered, and Lewis had deliberately avoided any explanation. But he seemed perfectly normal, sound of mind. The same boy as she'd known from school.

And like before, he kept things secret from her now, never really letting Becky into his life.

What was he hiding from her?

Chapter Twelve

Lewis paced around in his bedroom, unable to sleep. The meeting with Becky had played on him all day, and with the advent of darkfall, his fears grew even stronger.

What was he to do? It was a terrible situation, all paths before him looking grim. *Should he hope for the best, that they would leave him alone?* He shook his head. If Becky was right, then Grant and the others would eventually come looking for him. Maybe just to ask questions, but knowing the man's adamant character, this possibility seemed increasingly doubtful. That confrontation must be avoided at all cost. There was nothing within his power to stop what would certainly happen...

He gazed around the room, wondering.

It was close by. It always was.

Lewis didn't need to see it, to know this for a fact. He felt the invisible presence. Somehow, they were attuned to each other. And he also knew, that if he were to look outside his window, this fact would be proven by the sight of a pair of eyes watching him from below.

How had he ever come to accept this as part of his life? His routine? It was unthinkable.

But the answer came swiftly to him -- because it had *become* normal through the passing of years. Something so incredible, which defied understanding. Lewis had no idea where the thing came from. What it even *was*. Or why it never left, instead warding him with a terrifying vigilance. Unyielding, with a singular purpose.

Protecting him.

He'd even become used to its physical appearance, which was nothing short of monstrous, in both size and description. It was a wonder that he hadn't died of fright the first time he saw it. The creature was a behemoth, powerful and terrible. He shuddered in recollection.

And there was no real communication. No conversation. He could ask a million questions, and his reward would be only a blank stare. He had tried in the past. Asked about its motives, why it lingered, constantly with him. Told the creature to go away, thanking it for saving his life and looking after him.

All to no avail. The thing was mute, silent and immovable. It was like speaking to a mountain, and telling it what to do.

Lewis had tried in the past to make it react, always with no result -- except for now, this one incident with the children. Lewis commanded, and it acted immediately. To be honest, he had always secretly wondered about this. Sequestered away in the back of his mind, he'd been curious as to how much control he could exert over his invisible companion. His assumption had been that it would listen to everything he told it.

Why else would it bother to keep him safe from all harm?

But another part of him slunk away from this possibility. It was there for a reason, but maybe the real reason was yet to be revealed. *And if it failed to obey his wish, what would be the repercussions?* This idea bothered him greatly, and Lewis purposefully had avoided any situation where he might be tempted to call upon its power, or to unleash its wrath. The consequences would be horrendous.

No. Lewis had no desire to feel such power within his own hands, and *that* was perhaps the most harrowing of all possibilities -- that it *wanted* him to command it, and let loose a cyclone of violence and destruction that would have no end. Perhaps that was its hidden purpose.

No, it must not happen. Lewis would do everything possible to make sure these theories were never put to the test.

It was truly unthinkable.

He slumped onto his bed, feeling incredibly weary. He would decide a course of action soon, and move on it. If he needed to leave his home, then he would be up to the task. *Anything* to avoid a possible confrontation with Grant and the townspeople. Misguided or not, they had touched upon a measure of truth concerning his behavior, and why he kept to himself -- to avoid bringing anyone else into his personal hell and protecting others from the monstrous thing which warded over him, and would surely keep him from harm.

Despite his good intentions, there was simply no plausible way to tell the truth. He dared not give away his secret, for fear that the creature would react, determining such an action as a threat to his welfare. He would miss his home, and he would miss Becky as well. They'd spoken little over the past few years, but he thought about her often, and they would exchange a smile whenever they chanced to meet in town somewhere. But she couldn't become embroiled in the chaos of his life. She deserved peace of heart and mind, and the safety of her friends and family.

It was decided then. Tomorrow he was going to leave. Pack up his belongings, take his savings, and head north. Find some high country far removed from others, where he could live out his life without the threat of intrusion. He had been alone for a long time, and already knew that he could get by this way.

Well, not entirely alone.

Lewis lay down and turned off the lamp on the bed stand, closing his eyes and trying to rest unsuccessfully, but nearby in the outside darkness were another pair of orbs -- bright yellow, watchful and unsleeping.

Chapter Thirteen

Grant was restless.

His heart was heavy, his chest tight with anxiety as he worried about the upcoming task at hand, and what would have to be done. What *needed* to be done. To protect his family, his friends, and the townspeople. And himself, of course. Because whatever lived up there with Lewis was inhuman, an abomination against everything that was good in this world. He didn't know the true nature of that thing, and didn't want to. But he knew it was evil, despite the action to save the children. It was a front, a false face, and that was how the devil worked. In terrible, wicked ways. This was all preparation for worse things to come, the groundwork for a foundation that would ultimately spread out, let its poison seep through their community and ravage them all, physically, and more importantly, spiritually.

He wasn't going to let it happen.

There was a battle being waged here, the oldest one known to mankind. Good against evil. It was that simple.

Checking the ammunition cartridges, he wiped down the barrel stock on the rifle, looked through the scope. He was an accomplished hunter, but he did so to help feed his family. He didn't believe in killing anything for sport, but only to eat. He'd shot many animals over the years.

To this point, though, he had never aimed his gun at a man. Grant had never killed someone before.

Soon, this would change.

It was not an easy decision, and he was torn inside. He feared Lewis, and what he could do. What that *thing* could do. But he also figured that if he could take him out quickly, before he even had a chance to know what was happening, it would be over. His hold over the monster would be broken, the creature forever banished back to the netherworld where it had come from. *Lewis* was the key. He was the master of the beast, controlling it somehow.

Grant sat down on a swivel stool, laying the weapon on the table top in his den. He poured himself a drink from the bottle of Jim Beam, downing it without hesitation. Soon it would be time to round the men up, gather them together to discuss the final plan. It stank of an old fashioned lynch mob, he knew, and that bothered him slightly. But that *thing* was up there with Lewis, and had to be destroyed. He knew it was a grave sin to commit the act of murder, a wicked deed, but he understood that there were exceptions, and this was surely one of them. He also believed in being tested, and if there ever was going to be one in his life, well, this had to be it.

His nerves were in overdrive, and the liquor didn't seem to have helped. He poured himself another drink, sipping first, and then downing it whole. He was someone who could handle his alcohol, and a few tumblers were nothing to him. He stood up and went over to the phone, dialing Pete's number.

After several rings, a husky voice answered.

"Yeah?"

"It's me."

"Grant." Pete was silent for a few moments.

"You there?"

"Yeah."

"You know what's gotta' be done. And soon. Tomorrow night. We talked about it, agreed on it. So now it's time to do what needs to be done."

"I know, but…"

"But what?"

"Well, Grant, I'm scared to death. We're all scared to death. By that thing up there with Lewis. Maybe it's done, and will leave us all alone."

"Done? Are you a damned fool?" Grant pounded on the wall. "Trying to back out now? This is our chance, before anything else happens."

"But…" Pete started, but was cut off.

"But *nothing*! Hear me out. Again…if we don't hit it first, then we'll all be sitting ducks, easy meat for when that monster comes creeping down out of the hills, under cover of night, and takes us all out. One by one. You've seen it. Tell me, Pete. You think it'll stop with just us? Do you want something like that hellish thing coming after your Gail? Our families are all in danger because of what we saw. This isn't about you and me, and the rest of the guys. It's about our wives and children. Everyone who lives in this town."

Grant listened, and could hear Pete's heavy breathing over the receiver. He'd struck a chord, and he knew it.

"Now I'm going to ask you once again, are you

with me or not? Because I'll say one thing more." He paused for effect. "If I have to go up there alone, against Lewis and that thing, I will. I swear I will. And if I fail, then Lewis will know exactly who else is involved. He saw *all* of us there at the river. Why do you think he hasn't been in town since then? And he'll send that creature down from the hills after you and the others. You'll be a dead man. Torn to pieces. And another thing I'll say yet…if I have to go up there alone and take him out myself, after you backed away?"

"What are you talking about?" Pete asked, his voice trembling.

"You're *still* a dead man."

With that, Grant hung up.

There, it was settled. Pete would fall into line, and if he did so, the others would follow. The same way that it was back at the plant. The same way as pretty much anywhere else, for that matter. The men would grumble and complain at times, speaking to each other on subjects which bothered them, but it never went any further. That's what made them followers, and Grant a leader. Both at work and in the community. He was a thinker, and took action once his mind was made up.

The others, well, they needed direction. Just like now, although none of them could claim anything in their experience which could compare with their current predicament. This whole situation was unbelievable, like something straight out of a horror movie, and Grant didn't care to watch that kind of thing. He didn't like all the gore and violence.

He looked over at his gun again, wondering what it would feel like once he pulled the trigger. Remorse, satisfaction, and relief? The taking of a life would be difficult, hell, the toughest thing he'd ever done. But he had to consider the larger picture, and realize that Lewis was something different, something evil. The devil wore many guises, it was said. And nothing more deceiving than the human form, but this time, he'd brought one of his own with him, straight from the vilest pit. Revealed himself a little bit too much, and that was all the advantage that Grant needed. He bit his lip, wondering if this was how they'd felt in Salem, when the Puritan judges rendered their verdict of condemnation on those accused of practicing black magic. Grant likened himself to those men, and had always sided with Cotton Mather and the judges, in the belief that witchcraft had been alive and well during those dark and troubled times.

The same as what was taking place now in his own small town.

Grant reached for the tumbler, pouring himself another drink. After downing it, he took the entire bottle in one hand, the glass in the other, and went upstairs. The hour was late, but he wasn't tired, his mind and body energized by the task which lay before him. Despite the alcohol, his head was clear, very clear, and no inward argument persisted, all of them defeated by his decision for action. If anything, his spirits were up, and he knew that once the act was completed, he would be able to rest easier, knowing that he'd done the right thing. It was a good feeling, one of power and righteousness, and it was all he needed to sustain himself for just a little bit longer.

Until tomorrow night.

In the living room, he looked at the TV, which was deep into some late night programming. He sat down on the sofa, drinking contentedly, his mind drifting from the previous darker thoughts and losing itself in the black and white oblivion of the old movie now playing. The characters looked increasingly fuzzier, the backgrounds becoming more realistic. His eyelids fluttered and he was now one with the film, interacting absurdly with the main character. It was an old western, and the town was drowning in a wave of crime and violence. The sheriff needed help, looking over at him, waiting for a sign of approval. Grant nodded. He was just the man to do it.

And as in all dreams, this one swirled about in a surreal vortex, as thought processes blurred and scenes changed, morphing from one strange setting into another, as Grant's subconscious mind waded through the chaos and confusion.

Wait, what was he thinking? How could the sheriff need his help?

He *was* the sheriff.

Chapter Fourteen

The woods were alive, the nocturnal creatures out on their nightly forage for food. A raccoon sniffed beneath a fallen log, the wizened black and white face smelling something interesting. Somewhere nearby an owl hooted, perched high in the forest canopy, hidden from view, its keen eyes missing nothing. Light vapor curled along the ground, seeping forth from a bog which was the central point of activity for this section of the hillside. A fox trotted by, coughing in agitation as it smelled potential rivals. Just as quickly it left, melting into the shadows.

The sky was clear overhead, glimmers of starlight finding cracks in the tree tops, the new leaves starting to grow thicker as the season warmed. There was a natural order to everything here, as basic and primitive as any other place in all the world. Hunter and hunted, predator and prey. That simple, that brutal.

The raccoon scraped away at the soft earth, finding something to its liking, and which could satisfy its hunger. Spiders and beetles scurried away, disturbed by the activity, reacting to the danger which threatened. Naturally persistent, the animal kept at it, furiously seeking out its evening meal, but suddenly the creature stiffened, freezing in place. Its heightened senses warned of trouble, and it stuck its nose in the air, trying to locate the source of hazard.

It couldn't smell, hear, or see anything, but still it remained alert, ready to bolt for cover.

And moving through the woods something *did* pass by, concealed but not unnoticed, a predator which far surpassed anything ever seen in this forest, or any other.

Chapter Fifteen

Like Lewis, Becky also had trouble sleeping.

Tossing and turning the night long, she had terrible dreams, filled with dark things chasing her. She was trapped within a particularly horrible nightmare, and she imagined someone screaming in terror, a high-pitched drone of pure fear. Becky clamped her hands over her ears, wishing herself out of the dream. She was helpless, not knowing where to go, what to do. She was cornered in some type of labyrinth, and the yells reached a crescendo. It was too much, her mind reeling, and she gasped out loud, realizing that she'd finally broken free from the shackles holding her unconscious.

Coming out of slumber, she escaped the dark prison which had held her close, and now hovered on the brink of full awareness, trying to shake off the cobwebs of fantasy.

But her horror reached a new threshold as she realized the screaming was still there, the echoes bounding along the corridors of her home...The nightmare had followed her from the dream, reached out with black claws and twisted its way into reality. Her reality. Someone was still screaming.

Wait, where was she?

The dream was over, and she had awakened. Confused for a moment, she recognized the familiar trappings of her bedroom -- the night stand, her dresser, the stuffed toys nestled again her pillows. Yes, she was definitely at home, in her house. And the screaming was coming from...

Here! Her own house!

She burst out of bed, tossing the blankets and falling to one knee on the floor, gathering her robe about her as she rushed into the hallway. Dawn was creeping into the shadowed home, but the faint glimmers of light held no hopeful promise as the cloak of fear was powerful, seizing her heart and mind. She heard the screaming, louder now.

The sound was coming from downstairs, and she nearly collided with her mother as she flung open her bedroom door, eyes wide in terror.

"Dad?" Becky asked.

Her mother's voice shook. "Grant?" Louder. "Grant!"

They both looked downstairs as a tremendous *crack* thundered from below, as if a train had left its track and come hurdling into the walls of their home.

What was happening? Were they having an earthquake? It was the only thing which made sense.

But the screaming...her father was downstairs.

Her mom reached for the stairway banister, but Becky grabbed her arm. "Wait, let me go first."

Her mother's face hadn't changed expression,

and she appeared to be on the edge of going into shock. Whatever was waiting downstairs, Becky *needed* to go first. In case…she didn't want to think about it. But something terrible had happened, and she steeled herself for the worse, trying not to let her imagination run wild.

She eased herself downwards, one step after another, her heart beating like a tribal drum echoing inside her head.

"Dad?"

She called out, her voice hoarse, barely a whisper. The house was silent, and she tried to see around the corner of the lower landing. Down she went, her scope of vision growing, and seconds later she reached the bottom, her eyes growing wider, taking in the destruction and chaos surrounding her -- the huge, gaping hole in the wall, plaster and drywall scattered everywhere. The shattered glass and broken table. The ruined TV, the overturned sofa.

And then she spotted what remained of her father, realizing that her imagination had fallen well short of reality…

Paul Melniczek

Chapter Sixteen

Lewis awoke early the next morning, blinking his eyes and rubbing the sleep away. Yawning, he stretched lean arms behind his head, reluctant to leave the comfort of his warm bed. Quickly dressing, he left his room and headed down the steps, a feeling of trepidation coming over him and growing stronger. Something seemed out of place to him. He paused in mid-stride. He immediately knew that something was wrong. Maybe *wrong* wasn't the right word. Different. And on any other day he might have been thrilled, shocked. Confused.

But now he was absolutely terrified, scared to the very bone...

The house was empty, the outside vacant, but his senses were the strongest indicator of all. He couldn't feel *its presence* anywhere. He was alone, *really* alone now, for the first time in many long years. There was no sign of his invisible companion.

What had happened? What was going on here?

Mouth open wide in shock, he grabbed the banister for support, pausing a moment before hurtling downstairs.

Impossible!

There was no sign of it anywhere. He looked about madly, trying to see, trying to feel...

But it was truly gone, and the implications were staggering.

He burst onto the porch, looking about in all directions. The landscape appeared normal and serene. Morning birds chirped from the meadow, excitedly caught up in their sing-song. A pair of rabbits dashed across the driveway, chasing each other in a mating ritual. A fat bumblebee landed on one of the bright perennials which encircled his porch, searching for precious nectar. The sun expanded its long arms, splashing the young day with golden warmth.

And Lewis was alone...

Beads of sweat trickled down his forehead, and cold, clammy hands crept along his back. His invisible companion, the unsleeping creature which protected him from harm, was missing.

It was gone!

Lewis almost yelled out, but knew it would have been a futile effort. After all these years, he'd grown used to its presence, despite not having the slightest idea of why it continued to remain at his side constantly. He had come to accept this as fact, realizing through time and trial that nothing would placate it.

And now...

It was gone.

Suspicions hammered down at him immediately, his instincts blazing in warning. His eyes gazed across the landscape, over the treetops, and downwards. Yes, he knew where it had gone, there was no question. And why it had gone. He ran back inside the house, grabbing the keys to his truck, a sinking feeling in the pit of his stomach knotting about, his mind screaming that it was already too late.

No! Not like this!

Lewis sprinted to the truck, jumping in and starting the vehicle, the engine roaring to life. In his haste, he forgot to release the emergency brake, his head swimming in dreadful possibilities. The vehicle stumbled and lurched down the road as he went dangerously fast, thinking only that he must get to town and warn the people. Call it off. And Grant? Becky's father was in the gravest peril. No harm must come to him or anyone else. He would tell them about, tell them...

Here he faltered. Tell them *what*? That something monstrous and unstoppable, his invisible protector, was coming after them now with deadly intent, striking first before they could move against him? This was the single thought going through his mind. It had to have known that they were plotting against him, and it was going to attack in a pre-emptive assault, one which would prove disastrous for those involved.

Fatal...

Thinking about it now, Lewis wondered if Becky's words had set it off, the creature listening as she warned him, or whether it was something else, its own unique intuition.

What did he really know about this thing anyway?

Nothing.

Absolutely nothing.

Where it came from, why it had come, and why he was the one it chose to protect, with a singular focus that was terrifying. The only things Lewis did know, were the fact of its existence, and its vigilance of warding him from harm. That was it.

He slammed his hand against the steering wheel, cursing his luck and life. Why *him* of all people? To what purpose? Was there some reason behind these events, or would the answer remain forever unexplainable, a glitch in the universe, where he was simply swept up in fantastic circumstances in which he would never have a chance of changing, or directing?

Lewis didn't give up, though. Perhaps there was still hope to be found. Maybe he could call off his keeper, place himself in a position to defend the chosen victims. It seemed fragile, but there it was. It was all he had left.

The minutes dragged by like an eternity, and eventually the forest grew thinner as he descended. Before him, silhouettes slowly grew larger, the angles and blocks turning into buildings and other structures, the concrete fabric of his hometown. And it was in terrible danger, all because of *him*. Perhaps not directly, but due to his lack of foresight and any subsequent action. Lewis had hesitated, and that indecision might prove disastrous. If he would have acted sooner, moving away immediately, then perhaps the creature would have let things go. His mind raced with all the possibilities, and it changed nothing at all. He didn't feel that he was in any danger himself, but Grant and the townspeople? *They* were not being protected by a monstrous entity.

The road forked and he plunged into town, reaching the end of Main Street, but he felt an ache in his chest when he saw police cars swarming all over, their sirens flashing like the eyes of angry dragons. It was a scene of turmoil, people in the streets and sidewalks, the townsfolk awakened early to events which had disturbed them.

The Unseen

Too late, Lewis thought.

I'm too late...

Mechanically, he headed towards Becky's house, which was located several blocks down to the left. He pleaded to himself that he was wrong, that nothing had happened to Grant or anyone else. As he neared her place he slowed as a small crowd of people were gathered about, pointing and shaking their heads. Lewis parked to the right, avoiding the stern-looking policeman directing traffic and dealing with curious onlookers.

Lewis stepped out, first moving briskly, and then running full toward the house. He spotted the gaping hole which had once been the front of the home, and his mouth opened wide. He was stunned by the destruction. An ambulance was double parked, and a pair of paramedics appeared in the background, carrying a stretcher between them, moving toward the vehicle. Lewis visualized Grant's stubborn face in his mind, and what it would look like in death. His worst fears had materialized.

His keeper had unleashed its wrath.

And Grant?

Lewis was certain that he was dead, and that it was his lifeless body which was now being taken away. He knew it. But still, he *had* to see for himself, although the guilt would never be purged away at this point. Ignoring the officers, he pushed right up to the paramedics, searching for a glimpse of the man they carried and the dread confirmation that would ensure his terrible lack of foresight, his ultimate failure...

They swept alongside him. "Make room now, out of the way! Please!"

Lewis looked down...

...and instead of seeing Grant's taciturn demeanor, he recognized Becky's pale face in her father's place.

Becky! No!

He stumbled back, his mind and heart overcome with anguish, but her eyes opened as they passed Lewis, and they locked stares.

"Watch it, she's in shock. Give us some room." One of the men gave Lewis a sharp look, another attendant opening the rear door of the ambulance.

Lewis was stunned, and he gasped for air, shaking his head. "She's all right? Becky, I'm sorry, so sorry…"

She whispered. "Lewis, you promised me that no one would be hurt. My father's…dead."

Grant was dead. And yes, he had told her that the people in town would never be hurt. But in the end, he had lied, and her father was now dead because of it.

The paramedics took her inside. Lewis watched as tears ran down her gentle face, and she held up a hand, which slipped down over the edge of the stretcher.

"It wasn't my fault, Becky. I'm so sorry."

The ambulance door closed, and with it, any shred of hope that Lewis still had left. He watched the vehicle lumber away, the siren wailing into the morning sky which had appropriately clouded over. A small crowd waited, several of them witnessing the strange scene.

And then the first murmurings began to circulate through the crowd.

"…Lewis. What's he doing here? He was there at the bridge, they said."

"Did you hear what she told him?"

"His fault? Lewis had something to do with this…"

Lewis heard all the accusations. He stood there, arms hanging limply at his side. He was the picture of guilt, and guilty he was.

The Unseen

The crowd was growing restless, the comments becoming harsher.

"I always thought he was no good..."

"They saw that thing, did you hear them? Said he's evil."

"... a monster in the hills. Demon."

"Officer!"

And just like that, things had become deadly. It was time to act. To hesitate now would cause even more death, and that was the last thing Lewis wanted. Moving purposefully away from the crowd, he turned to leave. And then he spotted something huge coming toward them from across the street.

No...

Lewis sprang away, heading for his truck. People shouted that he was trying to escape, and in reality they were telling the truth, but he wasn't escaping just from them -- he was running from his past, present and future, and the terrible fate which held him fast, refusing to let go.

His movement caught the attention of the police officers, who were now eyeing him suspiciously, several citizens pointing at Lewis and shouting. He reached his truck unhindered and started the engine just as a tall policeman trotted towards him with a hand raised in the air. Lewis ignored the man, instead focusing on the large shape of the monstrous creature which moved steadily toward them both, unseen by any but himself.

Lewis tore into the road, ignoring the yells and hand waves, spinning his tires and screeching down Main Street in the opposite direction. Everything was closing in on him, and he felt the pressure as a physical thing, squeezing him relentlessly into oblivion. His options had run out...The creature would continue to follow him wherever he went. Basing this on what it had done in the past, and what he believed the future held for them both, it was just something he *knew*. It was a part of him, latched on by some unseen connection, as invisible to him as the monster was to everyone else.

Reason had nothing to do with any of this.

His reality was a black nightmare -- worse than a nightmare, because there was no hope of waking.

He raced through town, hearing sirens pursuing him. Houses and businesses passed him on either side, his old stomping grounds which he could never be a part of, never be accepted, especially after these terrible events and Grant's death. Lewis wondered if there were others involved? More people who plotted against him? If so, they were all in danger. Maybe the creature had found them already, and killed them as they slept.

Lewis was devastated. Flight was the only way out, for the sake of everyone here. If the creature perceived a threat against him, it would act first. This was a battle the townsfolk could not fight, and he was the key, their only hope for survival. They would try to pin Grant's murder on him, despite the lack of physical evidence. And now he had no idea who else had suffered Grant's fate. Becky might recover from her own anguish, but what about the loss of her father? Maybe her mother as well?

Emotion tore through Lewis, ripping apart every fragment of his being. He had tried, oh how he had tried...living on his own, isolating himself from the community. Protecting them. But in the end, he had failed. Blood was now on his hands, regardless of never having raised a hand. It didn't matter. He was unique, and he had a special responsibility to the people surrounding him, the entire world, because of the power he held within his grasp -- one in which he could either wield or hold back.

Lewis wept, giving into despair, the tears finally coming to him. They flowed down his cheeks and onto his lips. He couldn't remember having cried in years. Somehow, he'd always accepted his fate, coming to terms with something which defied his understanding. And hope…had he ever felt there was any for him? Not really. He'd continued living across the years, moving from one day to the next, with no future before him, just the inescapable present. It was cruel, unjust, but it was also the undeniable fact of his life. And since no one else could change his life, undo the events which had led him to this place and time, all the responsibility fell upon his own shoulders to do the right thing.

Lewis had failed…Becky, Grant, the townspeople, and himself. They were all victims now. *His* victims. He couldn't even blame his unseen protector, because it reacted to his own actions, and the choices that he made.

He looked into his rearview mirror and saw two police cruisers following him, a large shadow trailing them even now. The officers would catch him soon. And then his companion would catch *them*. There was no doubt in his mind as to that outcome.

Lewis reached the edge of town, never slowing down. The road had been blocked off here, leading up to the bridge. The rest of the structure would soon be taken down and eventually rebuilt. *Here* was the spot at which fate had forced its hand on him. This had been the beginning.

And now it would be the end…

Several construction workers stood to the side, one waving an orange flag for him to stop. Instead, Lewis accelerated.

There would be no more blood on his hands. It was too much for anyone to live with.

But not to die for…

He would sacrifice himself to save more lives.

The truck crashed through the barrier while the

men shouted in warning. Lewis felt the wheels scrape for purchase, but within a few short yards there was nothing but air beneath them. The world began to turn, first sideways, then upside down in a dizzying spin. Colors raged before his eyes -- the murky gray of the sky, the healthy green of meadows, the dark blue of cold water. The truck glided across the air for several seconds, then nosedived toward the water.

Lewis thought of his parents, both long gone.

Soon they would be reunited...

Becky... the potential for something special.

Maybe in another time, another world...

He braced himself for the coming impact, hoping it would be over quickly.

Please forgive me, I didn't know...

The construction workers stared down, shocked by the horrific scene, unable to understand why the man had driven across the devastated bridge. They were helpless to do anything, some of them already pointing downriver to attempt a rescue, although the truck had been barreling along when it hit the blockade. They shouted, their voices filled with terror.

Confusion.

And then amazement, as the truck stopped inches away from the water as if some unseen force held it impossibly above the river, halting its deadly descent, then quickly moving off and taking it swiftly away downstream.

The men were stunned, some exchanging glances and others swearing, but all of them feeling the cold hands of dread squeezing mercilessly at their hearts, as they were touched by something well beyond their comprehension. The terror held them rooted to the scene for long moments, the event marking them all for the remainder of their lives.

And more than one of them would swear

afterwards that the man inside the vehicle -- identified later as Lewis fleeing from town -- had pounded on the glass, but whether it had been from relief or horror, none would ever know, for both truck and occupant were never seen again.

The End

Paul Melniczek

About the Author

Paul Melniczek is the author of 19 books, and has been writing for over a dozen years. He has sold over 100 short stories to a variety of markets, including the DARK SIDE mass market series of anthologies (ROC Books), FANGORIA, CEMETERY DANCE, DARK DISCOVERIES, SPACE & TIME, HIGH SEAS CTHULHU, HORRORS BEYOND, the SHIVERS series, and many others.

His titles include A HAUNTED HALLOWEEN, MONSTERS, OGRE'S PASSING, THE ROOTING OF EVIL, THE SUMMONING, THE CELEBRATION, MISCHIEF NIGHT, THE WITCHING HOUR, CHILDREN OF THE NIGHT, THE WATCHING, WHEN THE LEAVES FALL, DARK HARVEST, A HALLOWEEN HARVEST, TROUBLED VISIONS, BAD CANDY (with Al Sarrantonio), THE UNSEEN, SHADES OF LOVECRAFT, RESTLESS SHADES, and FRIGHTFUL OCTOBER.

Some of his publishers include Dark Regions Press, King's Way Press, Bad Moon Books, Cemetery Dance, Double Dragon, and Sideshow Press. He writes primarily supernatural and fantasy fiction, and some of his work falls under the YA category. He's been called a modern traditionalist, and firmly has his roots in classical fiction.

If you enjoyed THE UNSEEN, make sure to check out his other works available on Amazon, B&N, and most major online booksellers.